Where's Glimmer?

Don't miss any of Bella
and Glimmer's adventures!

Unicorn Magic

Coming soon

Unicorn Magic

- BOOK 2 -

Where's Glimmer?

BY JESSICA BURKHART

Illustrated by Victoria Ying

Aladdin

NEW YORK LONDON TORONTO SYDNEY NEW DELHI

ALADDIN

An imprint of Simon & Schuster Children's Publishing Division
1230 Avenue of the Americas, New York, NY 10020
This Aladdin paperback edition August 2014
Text copyright © 2014 by Jessica Burkhart
Cover illustrations copyright © 2014 by Victoria Ying
Interior illustrations by Victoria Ying
All rights reserved, including the right of reproduction in whole or in part in any form.
ALADDIN is a trademark of Simon & Schuster, Inc., and related logo
is a registered trademark of Simon & Schuster, Inc.
Also available in an Aladdin hardcover edition.
For information about special discounts for bulk purchases, please contact
Simon & Schuster Special Sales at 1-866-506-1949
or business@simonandschuster.com.
The Simon & Schuster Speakers Bureau can bring authors to your live event.
For more information or to book an event contact the
Simon & Schuster Speakers Bureau at 1-866-248-3049 or
visit our website at www.simonspeakers.com.
Cover designed by Jessica Handelman
Interior designed by Mike Rosamilia
The text of this book was set in Arno Pro.
Manufactured in the United States of America 0714 OFF
2 4 6 8 10 9 7 5 3 1
Library of Congress Control Number 2014936192
ISBN 978-1-4814-1106-6 (hc)
ISBN 978-1-4424-9824-2 (pbk)
ISBN 978-1-4424-9825-9 (eBook)

BE YOURSELF.
IF YOU CAN'T BE YOURSELF,
BE A UNICORN.

Acknowledgments

So much gratitude to the amazing team at Simon & Schuster. First, I have to thank Alyson Heller, Editor of All Fantastical. Aly, you waved a magic wand over Unicorn Magic and also shared your wand with me. I wouldn't have written a fourth of the fabulous fantasy elements had it not been for you. You taught me a new way of writing, and I'm so grateful. Your aura is bright purple!

Thanks to Fiona Simpson, Bethany Buck, Mara Anastas, the sales reps, and everyone at Simon & Schuster who worked so hard on *Where's Glimmer?*

Special thanks to Rubin Pfeffer for handling everything businessy so I can write.

Victoria Ying, again you've created a dream cover!

Finally, thank *you* for reading all about Bella and Glimmer! I hope you like their latest adventure. ☺

Contents

Where's Glimmer?

1

Glimmer + Bella 4Ever

"Glimmer!" Princess Bella yelled before she burst into giggles. The princess's unicorn picked up the brush from Bella's hand and held it in her mouth. The shimmery white unicorn shook her head, sending her purple-tinted mane flying. It was like she was teasing Bella. "Are you excited because it's Saturday and I have all weekend to spend with you?" Bella asked.

"She's sneaky," said Ben, a boy only a few years older than Bella. Glimmer reached out her muzzle, offering Ben the brush. He took the brush, grinning. Ben had arrived a couple of days after Bella had been Paired with Glimmer. He was the nephew of Frederick, the stable manager, and he had come from the neighboring kingdom of Foris as an apprentice of his uncle. It was up to him to teach Bella about unicorn care and riding. More important, he had been assigned to help Bella and Glimmer prepare for their upcoming Crystal Kingdom debut.

It was a beautiful, sunny day in Crystal Kingdom, the land ruled by Bella's parents, King Phillip and Queen Katherine. The air smelled like honeysuckle and roses. Ben had secured Glimmer to a post just outside the royal stables with a shimmering rainbow-colored rope that was also used to help lead her around. Bees and butterflies flitted through the air, looking like confetti. A few of the bees flashed neon yellow, almost like a flashlight being turned on and off. That meant the bees had sensed pollen in the air and were headed toward a sweet-smelling flower.

The butterflies in Crystal Kingdom were more beautiful than any others in the neighboring kingdoms. Crystal butterflies had wings lined with teensy sparkles that flashed and glittered like diamonds in the sunlight.

"Thank you for showing me how to keep Glimmer clean, Ben," Bella said, lifting her hand to shield her eyes from the sun. She eyed Glimmer— her very own unicorn—who had been a gift on her eighth birthday. A gift per royal tradition, of course. The unicorn's coat was super shiny, and her mane and tail were silky after Ben had helped Bella comb them.

"No problem, Princess Bella," Ben said.

"Ben, please," Bella said. "Just call me Bella."

"Okay, Prin—I mean, Bella." Ben smiled at her.

"Do you like taking care of the unicorns?" Bella asked Ben.

Most people did not have a unicorn. It was law

3

in Crystal Kingdom and the surrounding kingdoms that the best unicorns were saved for the royal stables. Other unicorns ran free, and it was against the law for a commoner to capture one.

Ben laughed, looking at Bella. "I love it," he said. "Uncle Frederick has taught me so much already. I don't know much about the royal customs, but I do know about unicorns."

"Did you know someone royal in Foris?" Bella asked.

"My father worked in the royal stables at Foris Castle," Ben explained. "He had been training me so I could work in the stables someday too. But he broke his arm a few weeks ago working with a royal unicorn."

Bella's long brown hair swirled around her shoulders as she whipped her head around to look at Ben.

"Ouch! I'm so sorry! Is your dad going to be okay?" she asked.

Ben nodded. "He'll be back in the stables in a couple of months, but he didn't want me to lose any time. Uncle Frederick has been training and caring for unicorns even longer than my dad, so I'll be living with him until my apprenticeship is done."

Bella climbed the white fence and looked out over Crystal Castle's grounds. She loved watching unicorns frolicking in the lush pastures. But when Bella thought about the unicorns, it reminded her of her upcoming debut with Glimmer. It was going to be here so fast—this coming Wednesday morning! It was especially exciting because it was a holiday and there would be no school.

It was royal tradition that within the first month of a prince or princess being Paired with a unicorn, the pair presented themselves to the kingdom. Bella's parents had told her that the people of Crystal Kingdom were eager to see the princess and her unicorn. Bella couldn't wait to introduce Glimmer to the townspeople!

Bella shifted her gaze back to Glimmer as Ben climbed the fence to sit next to her. She'd only been Paired with Glimmer a week ago, but she loved her unicorn more than anything in the entire Crystal Kingdom (well, except her parents!). Definitely more than all of the people in the other three sky islands. Bella had learned in geography class that sky islands were pieces of land that floated high in the clouds. The only way to reach another sky island was to cast a spell to create a rainbow or moonbeam to walk over as a bridge between two islands.

"I can't believe I got so lucky," Bella said. Glimmer pointed her cute ears in Bella's direction. "My eighth birthday was so scary!"

"How do eighth birthdays work for princes and princesses?" Ben asked.

"Well, every royal is born with an aura," Bella explained. "It's this kind of light that shows when a royal turns eight and when they are crowned king or queen. It can be any color of the rainbow." She paused, frowning. "Except for red."

"So red auras don't exist?" Ben asked.

"Actually, they *do*. But if someone's born with a red aura, it's a very, very bad sign. Have you heard of Queen Fire?"

Ben nodded quickly. "My uncle warned me about her. He told me never to enter the Dark Forest and explained that Queen Fire was, like, your family's enemy."

"Actually, Queen Fire," Bella said, taking a big gulp of air, "is my aunt. She is the first royal in history to be born with a red aura." She squeezed her eyes half-shut, peeking at Ben through her lashes. *I hope I didn't scare him by telling him a crazy evil queen is related to me,* Bella worried.

7

"Whoa," Ben said. "I didn't know Queen Fire was related to you. My uncle didn't tell me that part. That must have been scary for you when you waited for your aura to appear."

"It was!" Bella agreed. "My mom's is green and my dad's is yellow. Once I learned about my aunt, I got scared that my aura might be red."

Ben laughed, his brown eyes twinkling. "I haven't known you that long, but there's *no* way your aura ever could have been red."

"Thanks, Ben," Bella said. "Only my best friends, Clara and Ivy, know Queen Fire is related to me. I hope you don't want to stop teaching me now that you know."

Ben reached out a hand to stroke Glimmer's forehead. "No way. No evil queen relative is going to scare me off from helping you with Glimmer." He grinned, a mischievous glint in his eyes. "You've got a lot to learn, Princess."

Bella laughed. "Oh, really? Well, I'm glad you're sticking around then."

"Let's take Glimmer for a walk, and you can tell me more about being a royal," Ben said.

Bella nodded, and Ben untied Glimmer, handing the soft rope to Bella.

The three set off down a familiar path that wound through the castle grounds and circled one of the castle's many lakes.

"My aura appeared during the Pairing Ceremony on the night of my birthday," Bella explained.

"A Pairing Ceremony is where you're matched to your unicorn, right?" Ben asked as he walked beside Bella.

"Yes. I got this strange tingly feeling, and a purple fog surrounded me. It was my aura. Your uncle Frederick asked me to walk in front of unicorns that he had picked for me."

"He told me a little about that part," Ben said.

"Each royal unicorn glowed, showing its aura, and you had to keep going until you found one that matched you, right?"

"That's right," Bella said. She, Ben, and Glimmer continued walking through the cropped grass toward the lake. "I was getting so scared that none of the unicorns would turn purple. Then I stepped in front of Glimmer, and it was so magical. She changed from white to purple in seconds!"

"That is *so* cool! I can't wait until I'm old enough to help during a Pairing Ceremony." Ben got a faraway look in his eyes, as if he was picturing himself in Frederick's place.

"I felt this instant bond with Glimmer," Bella said. She reached up a hand and patted the unicorn's neck as they walked. "I'd been dreaming about my eighth birthday my entire life, and Glimmer has made me so happy."

Glimmer snorted and bobbed her head.

"I think she's happy too," Ben said.

Bella, Ben, and Glimmer reached the lake. A spell had been cast on the deep water so it was clear enough that the bottom of the lake was visible. Bella and Ben led Glimmer to the lake's edge and halted her. Glimmer watched Ben and Bella peer into the water, then turned her own gaze to the lake water.

"Ooh, look!" Bella said. "See those spiky blue fish?" A school of electric-blue fish covered in spikes swam near the water's edge.

"Yeah! Look over there," Ben said, pointing. "There's a huge dog fish at the bottom of the lake."

Bella's eyes followed Ben's finger. It took a moment before she spotted the dog fish. The white fish had dozens of black spots and barely moved as it crawled along the lake's bottom. It had floppy ears that covered its gills, and instead of a fish mouth it had a dog's snout. Dog fish were important to lake life—they ate all the dirty algae and helped keep the water clean. Dog fish reminded Bella of vacuum cleaners.

Glimmer pulled on the rainbow line, stretching her neck toward the lake. Ben nodded his okay, and Bella let Glimmer lower her head and take a few sips of water.

"Want to try taking Glimmer for a ride tomorrow?" Ben asked.

"Really? Do you think I'm ready?" Bella asked. She clasped her hands together and tried very hard not to jump up and down.

"Definitely!" Ben said. "I think you guys are ready."

"Yaaay!" Bella cheered. Glimmer lifted her head from the lake, and water dripped off her chin whiskers. Giggling, Bella hugged her neck. "Silly girl. We get to go riding tomorrow! Our very first ride together."

"My friends Clara and Ivy are coming over tomorrow," Bella said to Ben. "They'll be so excited to see me ride Glimmer for the first time."

The trio stayed by the lake for a few more moments before starting the walk back to the royal stables. For the rest of the day, all Bella could think about was riding. It felt like her birthday all over again!

2

Better Than a Birthday

"Bella?" Bella's bedroom doorknob turned, and a girl with braided blond hair peeked inside. The girl smiled when she saw the princess. "Good morning."

Bella, sitting up in the middle of her already-made bed, grinned. "Lyssa! Oh, I thought you would never get here!"

The older girl looked at Bella's wall clock. The clock had a baseball-size pink crystal surrounded by twelve smaller crystals. Two light beams shot out from the center of the big crystal and formed clock hands.

"It's just after eight," Lyssa said, laughing. She

smoothed her gray skirt and teal blouse with pearl buttons. "I usually get here at this time."

Fourteen-year-old Lyssa had been Bella's handmaiden for more than a year, but she was more like a big sister. It was Lyssa's job to help Bella dress, get to the castle's schoolroom on time, complete all her homework, and assist Bella in any other way she might need.

Bella hopped off her bed and threw her arms around the older girl. "I know, but today's *special*!"

"Really? Spill!" Lyssa said, hugging Bella back.

The princess let go of Lyssa and looked up at her. "Ben said . . . I get to *ride* Glimmer today!"

"Oh, wow! Bella, this is so exciting!" Lyssa took Bella's hand and squeezed it. "Now I know why you already made your bed."

Bella nodded. "I already washed my face, too. I was waiting for you to come and help me pick out riding clothes before breakfast. Would you?"

"Hmmm." Lyssa tapped her cheek. "I don't know. . . ."

Bella made puppy-dog eyes at Lyssa.

Lyssa laughed. "Okay. I mean, I *guess* I'll help you." She flipped up the nearby light switch and opened Bella's closet door.

Both girls entered the walk-in closet. The bright-pink walls with a glitter top coat always made Bella feel cheerful. Racks of shoes were lined up along the walls, and Bella's clothes spun on rotating display racks. A crystal chandelier hanging from the ceiling cast tiny rainbows on the walls.

"Here are your clothes for riding," Lyssa said. "You'll need a pair of riding pants."

"How about the black ones?" Bella asked.

Lyssa grabbed the pants and long socks, and the girls moved to the boots.

"I think these will be perfect," Lyssa said. She held up a black pair of tall boots.

16

"I love them," Bella said. "It was so cool of Mom and Dad to get me riding clothes when I got Glimmer. Otherwise, I'd have to ride in jeans and sneakers!"

"That wouldn't be too bad, would it?" Lyssa asked.

Bella slipped into the socks and pants. "I didn't think so, but Ben said I had to wear a shoe with a heel. And not a high heel. A boot heel. I'll have to ask him why today. He did say jeans were kind of tight and uncomfortable for riding."

Lyssa walked over to Bella's T-shirts, nodding. "That makes sense. What color shirt, Bells? This will be a day you'll remember forever! Fashion choices included."

"Ummm." Bella rolled her eyes to the ceiling. "Purple! I want to match our auras."

Lyssa handed Bella a purple tee with a glittery heart in the center and a jacket with pretty buttons.

She held it up with a flourish, and Bella grinned.

Soon Bella was all dressed. Lyssa brushed her hair into a low ponytail. "I think you're ready to ride!" Lyssa said. "Have *so* much fun, and tell me every single detail when you're done. Promise?"

"Pinkie promise," Bella said. She locked pinkie fingers with Lyssa.

After checking to make sure everything was in place, Bella hurried down the long hallway and raced down the stairs to the dining room.

"Good morning, Bella," her mom said.

"Morning!" Bella said, sliding into her high-backed chair. She sat across from her parents at the long mahogany table.

Bella swung her legs back and forth under the table. *I don't know how I'm going to make it through breakfast!* she thought.

The glass pitcher of orange juice hovered over Bella's empty glass.

"Yes, please," Bella said.

The pitcher lowered itself closer to Bella's glass and tipped, and a stream of orange juice flowed into the glass. When it was nearly full, the pitcher righted itself and floated over to Queen Katherine. Bella's mom shook her head at the OJ pitcher and nodded at the silver coffeepot instead. The queen's dark-blond hair was in loose waves around her shoulders. She sat at the head of the table next to King Phillip. King Phillip, his brown hair almost the same shade as Bella's, sipped his cup of steaming coffee and smiled at her.

"Looks like you're dressed for something special," King Phillip said. His green eyes settled on Bella.

Bella, orange juice glass in hand, nodded her head so hard that juice almost sloshed over the rim. "Lyssa helped me," she said. "Ben said I needed to wear these special pants—breeches—if I was going to ride today."

"Ride, huh?" Queen Katherine asked. A hint of a smile curled on her lips.

"Yes!" Bella said, bouncing in her chair. "I didn't say anything last night because I was sure if I started talking about it, then I'd never stop. Lyssa drew me a bath with some kind of powder. . . ." Bella raised her eyes to the ceiling, thinking. "Oh! Lavender! She said it would help me sleep. I went straight to bed and tried not to think about Glimmer all night."

Both of her parents laughed. Bella gulped her OJ, finishing the glass in seconds.

"Did you manage to sleep?" her dad asked.

"Until five this morning," Bella said. "It felt like forever until Lyssa came."

"It's just a motherly guess," the queen said, "but you downed that glass of OJ in under a minute. Are you in a hurry to get to the stable?"

"Um . . . *yes*!" Bella said. "Plus, Ivy and Clara will be here soon. I'd already invited them over before Ben told me that I'd get to ride Glimmer today. They're going to be so surprised! All I told Ivy and Clara was to wear boots."

"Don't let us keep you," King Phillip teased. "But you must eat something for breakfast."

Bella stared down at her big empty plate. Eating was the last thing she wanted to do. Her toes wiggled in her new riding boots, and she rubbed her palms over her breeches. She sneaked a glance at her parents and let out a teensy sigh. They wouldn't let her leave without eating—not a chance.

The table, like every morning, was full from end to end with food cooked by the castle's chef. Platters that stayed heated were full of pancakes and waffles. Dishes were piled high with eggs and fruit. A stack of toast floated through the air and stopped in front of King Phillip.

"Two slices of honey wheat toast, please," the king said.

Two pieces of toast landed next to the scrambled eggs already on his plate.

Bella eyed the rest of the breakfast foods, deciding what would be the fastest to eat. "I'd like fruit," she said finally, staring at the bowl of mixed fruit.

The crystal bowl lifted into the air and floated toward Bella. "One scoop, please," the princess said. The silver spoon dug into the bowl of diced fruit and heaped a pile onto her plate.

Bella picked up her fork and speared a chunk of pineapple. She ate honeydew melon, watermelon, apple slices, purple grapes, cantaloupe, raspberries, and blueberries. In record time, the fruit was in her tummy.

The princess looked up at her parents. "Breakfast eaten," Bella said. "Can I go now? Please?"

Both of her parents eyed Bella's plate.

"Who's supervising your lesson today?" King Phillip asked.

"Ben," Bella said. "Frederick trusts him. Ben has tons of experience with unicorns."

"If Frederick thinks his nephew is capable of teaching you how to ride safely, then I'm not going to worry," Queen Katherine said, smiling. "Well, only a little bit."

King Phillip reached over and took one of Queen Katherine's hands in his own. "Don't forget that Glimmer isn't just any unicorn. She is Bella's protector and lifelong guardian. There's nothing in the entire kingdom that could make Glimmer hurt Bella."

The queen nodded. "You're right. I must remind myself of my first time riding Kiwi. He treated me like glass."

Bella pictured her mom's unicorn with green-washed mane and tail. Her father's unicorn, Scorpio, had a yellow mane and tail to match his yellow aura. Bella couldn't be happier to have a purple-washed unicorn to add to the royal family of guardian unicorns.

"Go ahead," King Phillip said. "Have fun and listen to Ben."

Bella pushed back her chair, the wooden legs making a scraping sound on the black-and-white marble tile. "I will! Thank you, thank you!"

She darted out of the dining room and hurried to the castle's front door. She pulled open the heavy wooden door and let out a tiny shriek.

"Sorry!" Ivy said, her hand raised to knock on the door.

"Great timing, Bells," Clara added, giggling.

"I'm so glad you're here!" Bella said. She threw an arm around each of her best friends.

The three besties balanced each other out. Quiet Ivy was a great listener. She had silky, straight blond hair that was cropped close to her chin. She was the one who often asked that Bella and Clara think about a plan before jumping into it. It had saved them from getting into trouble more times than Bella wanted to count!

Clara, taller than her two friends, had long, strawberry-blond hair. She had more energy than anyone Bella had ever met. In fact, Bella wondered sometimes if Clara secretly drank sugar water—gross!—in the mornings. Neither Clara nor Ivy cared about Bella's princess status, and that was exactly what Bella wanted.

"We wore boots like you told us," Ivy said, sticking out her foot. She had on ankle-high black boots with jeans and a T-shirt with a yellow butterfly.

"Good. Ben said it was for safety," Bella said, "in case Glimmer steps on our toes by accident. It would hurt a lot if we had on flip-flops."

The three girls hurried down the castle steps and started down the stone driveway. It was the time of morning where the weed zap spell was at work. The castle gardener cast a spell over Crystal Castle's driveway when night fell. The next morning any weeds that had poked up around the fountain or through the cobblestone driveway began to shrivel and shrink. When she was little, Bella used to sit on the driveway and watch the weeds pout and grumble as they disappeared back into the soil.

"I can't wait for you both to see Glimmer again," Bella said. "And to see me take her for a ride for the first time!"

Clara bounced as she speed-walked beside Bella and Ivy. "Me neither! Ivy and I just saw her last week, but it feels like forever."

"Are you sure you want us there when you ride Glimmer for the first time?" Ivy asked.

"Of course!" Bella said. "Why not?"

"Because it's a *huge* thing," Ivy explained. "I would understand if you wanted privacy. The bond you have with Glimmer is . . ." She paused, tilting her head. "It's so strong. I knew you were going to be linked through your aura match, but I've never seen anything love someone like Glimmer cares for you. It's like she's your best friend, guard, and very cool parent all in one purple package!"

The girls giggled, and Bella felt pride build up inside her from Ivy's words.

"That means so much, Ivy," Bella said, slinging an arm across her friend's shoulders. "I *do* want you and Clara with me today. It's a special day that I want to share with my best friends. Trust me, you're not the only one who is surprised by how fast Glimmer and I bonded. It sounds silly, but it feels as though she's been in my life forever!"

Clara and Ivy shook their heads.

"It's not silly!" Clara said.

"Now Glimmer *is* going to be in your life forever," Ivy added.

Ivy's words sent Bella into a sprint across the

stable yard. Suddenly she couldn't wait another second to be away from Glimmer. Ivy and Clara chased after her, and they skidded to a stop at the stable's entrance.

Bella forced herself to walk—no running allowed in the royal stables—and barely noticed the other unicorns' heads over their stall doors. The stalls had three high, glossy wooden walls that formed a box, and clean straw was spread over the floor. A single dazzling silver rope hung across each entrance. They were enchanted—only Crystal Kingdom royals or those who worked in the stable could remove the ropes and enter.

"Glimmer!" Bella called, as she reached the stall. "I'm here!"

But something was wrong. Bella blinked. And blinked again.

Glimmer's stall was empty!

3

Disappearing Act

"Where is she?" Bella wondered to Ivy and Clara. Her friends peered over the princess's shoulder into the empty stall. "Ben obviously already took her out."

But as she said that, she noticed Glimmer's magical rainbow-colored rope hanging limply on the stall wall.

"C'mon," Bella said. "Let's find them."

Bella turned away from Glimmer's stall, and her friends followed her back down the aisle. She ducked down a side hallway and headed for the storage area. The princess twisted the golden knob

on the door and sighed with relief. The dark-haired boy had a white, comfy-looking cushion hanging over his arm.

"Hi, Bella," Ben said with a smile.

"Hey, Ben," Bella said. "These are my friends Ivy and Clara."

Both girls smiled and gave little waves.

"We went to say hi to Glimmer," Bella continued, "but she wasn't there. Did you already take her out?"

Ben frowned. "Bella, I was here getting Glimmer's stuff. I haven't taken her out yet."

"You haven't?" Bella tried to swallow the panic that was rising in her throat. "Someone else must have. Glimmer's not in her stall! Where's your uncle?"

"Uncle Frederick took your dad's unicorn out for a ride," Ben said. "The other stable hands haven't arrived yet."

A small whimper escaped Bella's lips. The giant room seemed as if it was tilting. Bella felt as though she had eaten way too many pieces of chocolate cake and might throw up. If Frederick wasn't here and neither were the other stable hands . . .

"Glimmer's gone," Bella said in a whisper.

Ben's face paled. He put down the cushion, sidestepped around the girls, and headed into the hallway. "No," he said. "I saw Glimmer a few minutes ago. She can't be missing."

Ben, with the girls right behind him, hurried to Glimmer's stall. He stood before the stall entrance, mouth slightly open. His brown eyes seemed to darken as he picked up the rainbow rope and held it in his hand.

"Princess Bella," Ben said, bowing his head. "I must alert my uncle and the royal guards at once. Glimmer must have been kidnapped somehow. She was under my watch, and this is all my fault."

"No!" Bella said. She blinked back tears. "No one could have taken her! The magic rope won't allow it."

But what if Queen Fire somehow—No! Bella pushed the thought out of her mind.

"You and your friends should return to the castle," Ben said. "We will find whoever took Glimmer, Bella. I promise."

"I'm not leaving," Bella said. "Glimmer is my unicorn. I'm going to help find her."

Ben opened his mouth, as if he was about to argue, then closed it. "All right," he said. "When I go tell my uncle, he's probably not going to let me to come back."

"Why?" Clara asked. Her voice jolted Bella. She'd almost forgotten her friends were there.

"Because the princess's unicorn was captured under my watch," Ben said. "I'll likely be banished from Crystal Castle and sent home."

Ben started away from Glimmer's stall. His shoulders slumped, and he hunched forward as he walked. Bella squeezed her eyes shut, pressing her fingertips to her temples. Glimmer missing was too awful to think about, but she couldn't abandon Ben. He had been nothing but kind and helpful to her since his arrival. Bella couldn't stand the thought of him getting in such huge trouble that he would be *banished* from Crystal Castle forever.

"Ben, wait!" Bella called. "The monitors! We didn't watch them."

Slowly Ben turned back to Bella. "Monitors?"

"Frederick didn't teach you?" Bella asked, a flutter of hope in her chest. "Come back. Look." She pointed to a pearly button on the stall wall. "This will show us everything that's happened in Glimmer's stall in the last day."

"Wow," Ivy said. "Press it! Press it!"

"If we find out who took Glimmer," Bella said, "maybe we don't have to tell anyone. Ben, you don't deserve to get in trouble."

"But Bella, I do," Ben said. "Thank you for trying to help me, but I have to tell Frederick."

"Stop, you two!" Clara said. "We're wasting time! Bella, pull princess rank this *one* time and Ben has to listen to you. But only once."

Bella looked at Ben and shook her head. "I don't have to. Please, Ben? Try it my way first, and if we can't find Glimmer soon, you can tell your uncle."

Ben finally nodded. "Okay. But we only have until Wednesday morning's debut."

Without another word to Ben, Clara, or Ivy, Bella reached above her head and pressed the pearl button with her pointer finger.

"Royal monitor of unicorn Glimmer," Bella commanded. "Use your shine and use your shimmer. Show us the past, a day sped up fast. So we can see where Glimmer might be."

Instantly an image projected onto the wood. As if they were looking into a mirror, Bella and her friends gazed into the monitor's screen. It showed the previous morning, speeding through Ben feeding and watering Glimmer, taking her out of her stall to meet with Bella, tucking her in for the night, and then Glimmer eating dinner and falling asleep. But soon Glimmer woke and paced back and forth in her stall. Hours flew by of the pacing unicorn, who only stopped when Ben visited her this morning.

Then it happened. Everyone gasped.

"Monitor, rewind and slow down, please!" Bella commanded.

The screen faded to black. Then a clear image of Glimmer appeared on the wall. The purple unicorn poked her head out of the stall and looked from side to side, up and down the aisle. She put her muzzle over the snap-lock of the enchanted rope, and several moments later, the rope fell to the side of the stall.

Glimmer took in a deep breath, her nostrils flaring. She walked slowly out of the stall and down the aisle, and headed for the back exit. With a push against the wooden door, Glimmer squeezed through, and strands of her silky tail were the last of her caught on camera.

Bella dropped her hand from the button. She put her hand over her mouth, stifling a sob.

"Oh, Bells," Ivy said, grabbing her friend into a hug.

Bella started crying. Giant tears splashed onto Ivy, and sobs made Bella's stomach hurt. Clara rubbed the princess's back, and Bella fought to get her emotions under control. She was so upset that she wasn't even embarrassed to be crying in front of a boy.

"I—I'm so glad no one took Glimmer," Bella managed to get out a few minutes later. "I was afraid Queen Fire or someone had captured her. But—" A fresh wave of tears fell from Bella's eyes. "Glimmer *ran away*. She doesn't want to be my unicorn. All of this time I thought that she was happy, but she wasn't. Glimmer left to get away from me."

"Bella, that can't be true," Ben said. His voice was soft. "I've spent so much time with you and

Glimmer. She loves you as much as you love her. She would *never* leave you willingly."

"She did," Bella cried. "The monitors don't lie."

She slumped against Glimmer's stall. Clara, Ivy, and Ben sat around her.

"I think Ben's right," Ivy said. "Bella, think about how Glimmer acted last night. She was pacing and up almost all night."

Clara nodded, patting Bella's hand. "Something was wrong or upsetting Glimmer."

"*I* must have done something yesterday to upset her," Bella said. "Or maybe Glimmer's felt this way since we've been Paired, and she finally couldn't take it anymore."

"It *has* to be something else," Ben said. "We have to find Glimmer and figure out what's going on."

"I'll be worried until she's back in the stable," Bella said. "I want to start looking right away and keep it a secret. But once we find Glimmer—if we find her—I want her to be able to be free of being my unicorn if that's what she wants."

"Bella, let's find Glimmer first," Clara said. "Once she's safe and Ben's clear from getting into trouble, then we'll find out why she left."

Bella stood on shaky legs. Her heart actually hurt from fear for Glimmer's safety and the pain that her own unicorn didn't want her. *Just because Glimmer might not love me doesn't mean I don't love her*, Bella thought. *I'm so scared for her, and I won't sleep until I find her. I wish Glimmer knew how much I love her.*

"If we're going to keep this a secret," Ben said, "we have to act as though everything is normal. If my uncle comes to Glimmer's stall and asks where she is, I'll tell him that she's with you, Bella."

"I'll tell my parents and Frederick that Glimmer's with *you* if they ask," Bella replied.

Planning to return Glimmer to safety helped to

dash away some of her sadness. Instead of focusing on Glimmer's decision to leave, Bella decided to put everything she had into finding her unicorn. Once Glimmer was safe, then Bella would deal with letting go.

"I want to help," Ivy said.

"Me too," Clara added. "What can we do?"

"We have to start looking without appearing to anyone as if we're searching for anything," Bella said. "What if we all take sections of the castle grounds and search until it gets dark? If Glimmer escaped the grounds, then tomorrow we can map out sections of the kingdom to search."

"Don't forget school," Ivy said, frowning.

Bella groaned. "I forgot that tomorrow is Monday. Okay, *after* school we'll all meet up at the Snapdragon Garden."

"Are you sure no grown-ups will be there?" Clara asked.

"Positive," Bella said. "Yesterday I heard one of the gardeners tell my mom that the snapdragon flowers were especially mean this week. She told my mom to be extra careful if she walked through the garden, and Mom said she wasn't going to chance it."

"Oh," Clara said, her voice squeaky. "Okay."

Clara must have been picturing the towering flowers that filled Snapdragon Garden. They were beautiful, but their looks were deceiving. The flowers used their petals to nip at anything that got too close. The flowers couldn't breathe fire like real dragons, but smoke did come out of their mouths when they opened them if they were in a bad mood.

"We only have to go there if we don't find Glimmer today," Ben said. "She might be wandering close by."

Despite her churning stomach, Bella gave Ben a tiny smile. "I hope so."

"We need to get in touch with each other if we find her," Ben said. "Did everyone bring their crystal?"

Everyone nodded and reached into their pockets. They all took out smooth, quarter-size clear stones. The stones, nicknamed Chat Crystals, allowed the friends to send messages to each other.

"Let's cast a spell on them to vibrate and change colors depending on our message," Clara said.

"How about purple if someone finds Glimmer," Bella said. "Red if there is trouble and we need to get back to the stables immediately, and yellow if there's a possible trace of Glimmer and we need to help that person follow the lead."

"Perfect," Ivy said.

Bella held her crystal flat on her palm as her friends did the same. "Crystals, until dusk tonight, please change colors according to my words," she said, putting a spell on the crystals. Once she had finished, everyone tucked away their crystals.

The friends mapped out sections of the grounds and agreed to meet at the back of the stables at dusk. Ivy, Clara, and Ben gave Bella encouraging smiles before they all went their separate ways around Crystal Castle. Bella hoped the plan would work!

4

Search Party

Bella had been walking for hours, and there hadn't been a single trace of Glimmer. It was moments before dusk, and soon Bella would have to turn back to meet her friends. The new boots that Bella had so eagerly laced up this morning had rubbed blisters into her heels and big toes. Sweat trickled down her forehead and soaked the collar of her T-shirt.

Bella's crystal hadn't vibrated once. She had even taken it out of her pocket to see if she had missed a vibration, but the crystal remained clear. No one was having any luck.

Glimmer's definitely not in my section of the castle grounds, Bella thought. *But how did she escape the royal guards? Did she just walk across the drawbridge? Surely she could not have swum through the moat without being seen by guards.*

Bella forgot how lucky she and her friends were that none of them had been spotted by the royal security team. They would have to lie about what they were doing, and Bella hated lying. But this was for a good reason.

The princess took a few more steps and stopped as she reached the creek in front of her. Bella had taken the front left quarter of the castle grounds. Ben, Ivy, and Clara had each taken another quarter of Crystal Castle's grounds. Bella's section included a creek that had a small waterfall at the start. Even though her instinct told her that Glimmer couldn't have made it across the moat, she knew she had to try.

This is the last place left to look, Bella thought. *Then I have to get back.*

She sat down on the grass near the creek bed and undid her boots. She tugged off her socks, rolled up her pant legs, and stepped into the cool water. The creek bottom was covered in a bed of smooth brown and black stones—none sharp enough to cut or bruise Bella's feet.

Teensy minnows and tadpoles swam away from Bella as she carefully walked up the creek toward the waterfall. The ankle-deep water felt good on her blisters. The princess squinted and bent down, the setting sun visible in the water's reflection. *Something* had disturbed the rocks. The entire creek had been smooth and now there were—*one, two, three, four*—spots of rocks smushed into the ground. Bella stuck her hand in the water, tracing her finger over a U-shaped imprint.

Glimmer's shoe!

"Glimmer!" Bella called. She forgot that she wasn't supposed to be calling for the unicorn in case someone heard. She dropped her voice to a whisper. "Are you here?"

Bella stayed hunched over and followed the hoofprints as they went along the creek bed, then vanished. Steps away from the loud waterfall, she looked from side to side, trying to pick up the trail.

"The grass!" Bella said out loud. She sprinted through the creek, her footsteps spraying water up her legs. She put her bare feet in the spots of trampled grass—almost like playing hopscotch. The four diagonal prints zigzagged away from the creek and headed for the property line that divided Crystal Castle from the rest of the kingdom.

Bella slipped her fingers around her crystal. She needed to tell her friends to meet her here. The princess took a few more steps, and the hoof-prints became harder and harder to spot. A shiny screen that looked like plastic wrap was inches from Bella's face. The palm-size screen signaled the end of Crystal Castle land. Bella slowly put a foot through the screen spell, causing it to ripple.

"Princess? Princess Bella!"

Bella yanked her foot back as if it had touched scorching lava. She stifled a shriek and turned to the deep voice that had called her name. She released the crystal, leaving it in her pocket, glad she hadn't called her friends.

One of the members of the royal security team approached her. His sword gleamed at his side, and he was dressed in all black with a pin of the castle's seal on his lapel.

"Um, hi!" Bella said. She hurried away from the hoofprint trail and tried to scuff away the rest of the prints with her feet as she approached the guard. *I don't want him to see any of Glimmer's tracks*, she thought.

"Are you all right?" the guard asked after bowing to Bella. "It's not safe for you to cross the property line, Princess. The other guards and I only patrol the castle grounds unless the king instructs us otherwise."

Bella smiled. "I know. I was playing in the creek and then saw a"—she swallowed—"*butterfly*, and I chased it. I'd never seen one like it before. Thank you for calling to me before I went too far over the line."

The guard nodded, smiling back. His green eyes looked around as if searching for evidence of the butterfly. But he didn't seem to pick up on the princess's lie. "Of course, Princess. Do you need an escort back to the castle?"

"Oh no, thank you," Bella said. "I know my way from here. Thanks!"

Before the guard could say another word, Bella gave him a tiny wave and trotted away. She dashed across the creek, put on her boots, and darted across the grounds, hurrying back to the stables.

That was way too close! Bella thought as she jogged. *I have to be more careful.* Her stomach sank as she reached the stables. Ivy and Clara stood empty-handed and were covered in streaks of dirt. Ben came around the other side of the stables, red-faced and sneakers covered in mud.

"I knew that no one had found Glimmer," Bella

said, reaching her friends. "But I'd hoped my crystal had missed a signal."

The four of them plopped onto the floor of the tack room. Bella reached over and pulled a blade of grass from Clara's long hair.

"We don't have much time," Ivy said. "I have to be home really soon or my parents will worry."

"Mine too," Clara said. "I'm sorry, Bella. I looked *everywhere* in my section. I didn't find a thing."

Ivy and Ben nodded, their eyes downcast.

"At least you guys didn't get stopped by guards," Bella said.

"What?" Ben asked, sitting up straight. He'd been slouching against a wooden cabinet.

"I was in the creek and I found hoofprints," Bella said. "I know they're Glimmer's."

"Oh! Why didn't you message us?" Ivy asked. She swiped at sweat on her forehead.

"I started to," Bella said. "I got caught up following the prints. They led me to the castle line. I was halfway through the screen when a guard saw me."

Clara's mouth formed a giant O shape. "What did you do?"

"I had to lie," Bella said. "I told him that I was chasing a butterfly, and I ran off before he could ask me anything else."

Ben's brows knitted together. "Did he believe you?"

"Yes," Bella said. Her chest tightened a little. "I hated lying, but I had to."

"You did the right thing," Ivy said. She stretched her legs out in front of her. The knees of her jeans were grass stained.

"Now we know that Glimmer isn't on the castle grounds," Bella said. "The hoofprints pointed in the direction of the Dark Forest."

The mention of the Dark Forest caused everyone to fall silent.

"Guys," Bella added. "No one has to go in but me. I *have* to go—Glimmer's my unicorn. I understand if you don't want to go."

Ben shook his head. "No way. I'm going too."

Ivy and Clara nodded in solidarity.

"What if we start by searching around the castle after school?" Ivy said. "I'll tell my parents that I'm staying over for a while."

"I'll do the same as Ivy," Clara said. "If we don't find Glimmer tomorrow, then we'll go into the Dark Forest the next day."

Bella thought for a minute. "That's a good idea. Maybe we should be in pairs this time."

"I'll go with you," Ben said, looking at Bella. "If that's all right."

"Sure. Thanks, Ben," Bella said. "Ivy and Clara, are you okay going together?"

The two girls looked at each other and high-fived. "Team Clivy!" Clara said, giggling.

The overhead lights went from dim to bright. Bella looked out of the small window in the tack room. The sun was almost completely gone.

"You and Ivy still have to get home," Bella said. "I missed dinner, and I don't want Frederick to come looking for you, Ben. We will mess up this entire plan if we all get in trouble on the first day."

"You're right," Ben said. "Everyone needs to go."

"Tomorrow," Bella said. "Snapdragon Garden at two thirty."

5

Act "Normal"

After splitting up from her friends, Bella managed to shower and change clothes before running into her mom. The queen found Bella when the princess was drying her hair.

"When did you come inside?" Queen Katherine asked, folding her arms. Bella studied her mom's face. The queen wasn't angry, but she was definitely a little cross.

"I got in a while ago," Bella said. "I was sweaty and gross from being outside, so I took a shower. I didn't want to track dirt everywhere. I'm so sorry that I missed dinner, Mom."

"Did something happen during your riding lesson?" Queen Katherine asked. She raised a you-better-tell-the-truth "Mom" eyebrow.

"Nothing happened," Bella said. She hated lying to her mom. Queen Katherine trusted Bella, and the princess had never given her parents a reason not to trust her.

Until now. But she had to protect Ben and even shield Glimmer from trouble.

Bella had realized in the shower that Glimmer's decision to run away could get her unicorn into trouble. That was the last thing that Bella wanted.

"Everything went great," Bella added. "Ben was a great teacher. He told me to go after the lesson, but I decided to stay. I wanted to learn how to prepare Glimmer for bed after riding her." Bella stretched her arms behind her back. "It's completely my fault that I got in late," she added.

The queen eyed her, and Bella fought the urge to chew her bottom lip.

Please, please believe me, Mom, Bella thought. *I'm sorry I'm lying. I'll never lie again after this is over!*

"Next time, please make sure you send word that you'll be missing dinner," the queen said. "Don't make a habit of it, though, Bella."

"I won't," Bella promised.

Her mom smiled and stepped forward to wrap her arms around her daughter. "I am proud of you, sweetie. I remember my early days of learning to ride Kiwi, and it was quite tiring. I'm so happy you decided to stay at the stables and care for Glimmer."

"You could have just ridden her and left," Queen Katherine continued. "But you showed a true interest in Glimmer's well-being. That's my girl. Your father will be proud too."

The queen's words made Bella's stomach hurt.

* * *

On Monday morning, Bella was awake long before Lyssa arrived. She dressed herself, moving quietly so no one would know that she was awake, and settled onto her window seat. The events from last night ran over and over in her mind.

A swallow chirped outside her window and hopped on the ledge of the fountain. The bird dipped its head into the water, causing droplets to cascade down its neck and back. The little brown bird bathed in the early morning sunlight.

Last night, after the talk with her mom, Bella had eaten dinner and, claiming to be tired, had gone to bed early. She really had climbed under her covers before her usual bedtime, but she had been awake for most of the night. All Bella could think about was getting through school and searching for Glimmer. She would have to make certain that she didn't miss dinner for a second night in a row.

"Bella?" a soft voice called from the other side of the door.

"Come in," Bella replied. She pasted a fake smile on her face as Lyssa walked inside.

Lyssa's eyes swept over the already-dressed Bella. She tilted her head. "I know why you're up early. You can't keep secrets from me!"

What? How did Lyssa find out? Bella thought, panicked.

"Lyssa, you can't—" Bella started.

"Your ride with Glimmer went so amazing that you were going to sneak out before school to see her," Lyssa interrupted, grinning. "That's why you're up so early."

Lyssa's wrong—so wrong—guess made Bella snap her mouth closed. Relief swept over her that Lyssa didn't know the truth.

"You got me," Bella agreed cheerfully. "I was totally planning to see Glimmer. I got lost in a daydream, and now it's too late."

"Aw, Bells," Lyssa said. She smoothed her cheery yellow cap-sleeve dress. "The day will go by faster than you think. You'll be seeing Glimmer before you know it."

Bella managed a smile. "I hope so."

It was the first sentence of truth she'd spoken in a while.

Lyssa picked up a hairbrush and waved it at Bella. "Come over and let me do your hair," she said. "You have to tell me everything about your first ride!"

Slowly Bella uncurled her legs and walked across her bedroom. She sank into the plush pink-velvet-covered stool in front of her mirror.

Lyssa ran the brush through Bella's hair, locking eyes with her in the mirror. "Are you okay?"

Lyssa asked. The older girl frowned at Bella's reflection. "You're awfully quiet. I thought you would be dying to tell me about your day with Glimmer."

"Oh, I am," Bella said. "Yesterday was amazing, Lyss. I'm just a little tired and sore from riding."

Still brushing, Lyssa nodded. "I get it, Bells. I'm sure you were up the night before thinking about what riding Glimmer was going to be like. Then when it was over, I'm sure you felt like an energy zap spell had been cast on you."

"Exactly," Bella agreed. "Glimmer really does mean more to me than anything in my whole life, and I was so, so excited about yesterday." Under the vanity table, she curled her fingers into fists until her fingernails dug into her palms. It was all she could do to keep from crying. "She's the best unicorn in the whole world."

"French braid?" Lyssa asked, Bella's hair entwined around her fingers.

"Yes, please," Bella said.

"I'm so glad you're happy with Glimmer," Lyssa said. Her focus was on braiding Bella's brown locks. "I'll have to watch you ride sometime."

Bella managed a wobbly smile. "Sure."

Lyssa finished Bella's braid and knelt down by her side. "You know you can tell me anything, right? I can tell when something's bothering you. Are you worried about the Crystal Kingdom debut on Wednesday?"

I'm going to tell Lyssa everything, Bella thought. But then Lyssa would be in an awkward position. Enough people were already telling lies and keeping secrets—Bella didn't want Lyssa to be one of them.

"The debut is stressing me out a little," Bella answered honestly. "It's a big moment in front of the entire kingdom."

Lyssa patted Bella's knee. "It *is.* But you'll have

Glimmer there to support you. It's going to be so different from your birthday, when it was just you."

Bella tried to smile and nod as Lyssa kept talking about the debut. Not only was she worried sick about Glimmer, but what would happen if the princess of Crystal Kingdom showed up to her unicorn debut—*without* her unicorn?

6

Secrets, Lies, and the Dark Forest

The school day dragged. On and on and *on*. Bella, Ivy, Clara, and Ben all huddled together during lunch at a table on the terrace. Bella and the other students in her third-grade class were all taught at Crystal Castle. The princess's parents hadn't wanted Bella to be lonely, so they had invited children of castle employees to attend school with Bella and her tutor.

Today, however, Bella wanted to avoid everyone. While Ben was in school and away from the stables, he always told Frederick a different story about where Glimmer was. Today's little white lie? Ben had let Glimmer loose in a big field to graze.

"Does everyone have a copy of their map?" she said, whispering to her friends.

Ivy, Clara, and Ben, all seated at the round table, nodded.

"Last night I divided up the outside of the Dark Forest into sections," Bella explained. "Everyone's is marked, and I put a spell on the map to only reveal the ink of castle grounds. Just being extra careful."

"Good idea, Bells," Ivy said. Her short hair was clipped back with blue-and-white polka-dot barrettes. Ivy, preparing for the outdoor adventure, had paired sneakers with jeans and a dark-gray T-shirt. Ben, Clara, and Bella were in jeans and dark tees too.

"One question," Clara said. "How do we get past the royal guards?"

Bella rubbed her sweaty palms on her thighs. "I have an idea. What do you guys think about going to my mom after class and telling her that we would like to take Glimmer out in the giant field alongside the road to town?"

Ben rubbed his forehead. "I like it. We don't have to worry about the guards."

"Sounds like a plan," Ivy declared.

"Do you know more about the Dark Forest since the first time we talked about it?" Bella asked Ben.

He shook his head. "I didn't get a chance to read about it yet. Are there big spiders?"

"I wish," Bella said. "We might run into bigger problems than those eight-legged creepers. The forest is Queen Fire's territory. Her guards might be patrolling to keep us out."

Ben's eyes widened, and he nodded slowly, as if remembering Bella's confession about her relationship to Queen Fire.

"My aunt has been stealing unicorns for years," Bella said. "She uses her evil black aura to make all of the good unicorns become bad. And dangerous!"

"Will we be able to recognize them?" Ben asked.

"Easily," Bella answered. "They are red with black eyes." She stopped, her throat suddenly desert dry. She couldn't even begin to imagine what she would do if Queen Fire had captured Glimmer. Bella's sweet purple unicorn being turned evil . . .

"Hey," Ben said, nudging Bella's ribs with his elbow. "Queen Fire doesn't have Glimmer. I know it. Think about the way that Glimmer escaped her stall. She's too smart to be caught by Queen Fire."

"I hope so," Bella said. She picked up her silver fork and stabbed at a pile of macaroni-and-cheese noodles. The food tasted like nothing, and Bella put down her fork, pushing her tray away.

The four unicorn detectives spent the rest of lunch talking in hushed tones about how they were

70

going to track Glimmer, play it cool with Queen Katherine, and most of all, avoid the dangers that could pull them into the Dark Forest.

"Hi, Mom," Bella said. After school had ended, Ivy and Clara had waited for Bella to change into riding clothes. Then they found Queen Katherine in the downstairs library.

"Hello, sweetie," the queen said, looking up from the book in her lap. Queen Katherine smiled at Ivy, Clara, and Ben.

"Mom, is it all right if we cross the drawbridge and go into the field across from the castle?" Bella asked. She saw a frown begin to form on her mother's face. "It's Ben's idea," she added quickly. "He said taking Glimmer to a different setting to ride would be good for her. It will help prepare her for Wednesday, so she won't be so shy or frightened when we take her into town."

"Ben," the queen said, "is Glimmer comfort-able enough with Bella to be riding so far away?"

"Yes, Your Highness," Ben answered. "I spoke to my uncle Frederick about it, and he said okay. I *promise* that Bella will be safe."

"Please, Mom?" Bella asked. She tried not to notice Ben wringing his hands behind his back. "We'll be very careful. If I need you or Dad, I promise that I'll send for help via a spell." The queen looked from Bella, to Clara, to Ivy, to Ben. Her face gave away nothing. The queen placed her hands on her lap and smoothed her gold-and-rose-colored dress.

"Have fun," Queen Katherine said. "Be safe and come back in time for dinner."

"Thank you, Mom!" Bella said. "Bye!"

Before the queen could say another word, the friends dashed out of the library, through the castle front door, and toward the Dark Forest.

The guards shot Bella confused looks when

she reached the drawbridge, but she waved as she speed-walked by. "My mom knows we're going to the field," Bella explained.

The men and women dipped their heads and resumed walking back and forth across the drawbridge entrance.

"See you guys in two hours," Bella said, checking her watch. "We'll meet at the Snapdragon Garden unless someone messages the other with their crystal."

"Got it," Clara said. "That will give us plenty of time to get home for dinner."

"Hopefully, we'll be feeding Glimmer dinner tonight, Bells," Ivy said, squeezing her friend's arm.

With that, the friends split into pairs, and Bella and Ben headed for the part of the forest farthest from Crystal Castle. Neither of them spoke. They glued their eyes to the ground, searching for hoofprints, and walked to the edge of the forest.

It was a cloudless day in Crystal Kingdom, and sunlight fell on their backs. One look inside the Dark Forest made Queen Fire's territory live up to its name. Bella stopped, carefully keeping her toes in the grassy field, and squinted into the forest. It was as if the sunlight didn't extend to the wooded land.

"I can't see anything in the forest," Bella said. "Can you?"

Ben stopped walking and looked into the woods. "Just shadows," he said. "I don't want to think much about what's in there."

"What if Glimmer is?" Bella's voice shook a little. She couldn't stand the thought of her sweet unicorn in the scary Dark Forest.

Ben tilted his head, swiping hair out of his eye. "Let's just search our section. In a couple of hours, if no one's found anything, then we'll think about the Dark Forest."

"It's the only place left," Bella said, looking away from the forest. She started to walk again. The short grass grew tall and weedy. She stepped around a patch of burrs, and the prickly round seeds stretched their spikes as far as they could, trying to latch onto Bella's pants. "If Glimmer was loose in the kingdom, someone would have seen her and reported a royal unicorn sighting. The Dark Forest is *it*."

Bella bit down on the inside of her cheek to keep from crying. She had to stay strong for Glimmer and put her whole heart into searching for her.

And for the next two hours that's exactly what she did.

"Are you all right, Bella?" King Phillip asked. "You're so quiet lately."

Bella couldn't help but slump in her chair at dinner. The chef, Joseph, had prepared a delicious-smelling roasted chicken with plenty of yummy sides, but nothing sounded good to Bella. Not even her favorite mac 'n' cheese!

She and her friends had searched for two hours and met back at Snapdragon Garden. Not even one purple, sparkly hair had been found. Bella's friends promised they would be back tomorrow and they would go with her into the Dark Forest.

"I've been busy with school," Bella said. "I've been spending a lot of time at the stables with Glimmer, too. You know, getting ready for the debut."

Where I debut myself *alone!*

King Phillip peered at his daughter with kind eyes. "This society debut is nothing more than a royal formality. Please don't put too much pressure on yourself."

"I won't, Dad," Bella said. She speared a green bean and forced herself to eat it. "I promise."

"It's going to be nothing as grand as your birthday celebration," Queen Katherine said. "You'll ride Glimmer into town, and Dad and I will be behind you in the Royal Carriage. At the town square, you and Glimmer will stand next to the platform. You won't have to do anything, sweetie, if you're worried about that. This is a *very* informal event. It's just to let the townspeople see their princess and her new unicorn."

"That helps, Mom," Bella said. "Thank you."

Unless the event is canceled, the town is going to be staring at me, Bella thought. She tried to shake away the thoughts. *We are going to find Glimmer. We will.* She repeated the last sentence to herself over and over.

For the rest of dinner, Bella did her best to chat like normal. It felt like hours before the table was cleared and the princess was excused to go to her room. When her door was shut safely behind her, Bella crawled under her covers and cried.

7

Does Glimmer
Want to Be Found?

"We can do this," Clara said. It was just after school on Tuesday, and the girls had gathered to continue their search for Glimmer.

"I wish Ben could be here," Bella said. "He did the right thing, though, by not asking his uncle to let him skip chores and come with us."

Ivy nodded. "It's better that he didn't ask. We need zero suspicion on us."

Bella's gaze wandered ahead to the Dark Forest. The girls were only feet away from the edge of the forest.

"So let's stick with the plan we came up with,"

Bella said, looking back at her friends. "Ivy, you and Clara stick together, and I'll go alone." It was Bella's unicorn they were searching for, so the princess wanted her friends to be as safe as possible. If it weren't for Bella, they wouldn't be going into the Dark Forest.

Both of her friends frowned. They were not thrilled with Bella's plan. Clara and Ivy had both argued with Bella about the princess going alone into the Dark Forest.

"Please don't fight with me about it anymore," Bella pleaded. "I know you're both worried about me being alone, but I'll be okay. We all have our crystals in case we need to get in touch with each other."

Ivy and Clara exchanged looks.

"Just so you know—I'm not happy about this," Clara fretted. She pulled her long hair into a ponytail. "But I'm with you, Bella."

"Me too," Ivy said. She patted the pocket of her

jeans. "Promise us that you'll use the crystal if you even *think* you might get into trouble."

"Promise," Bella said. She took a long, deep breath. "Today is it." She didn't need to remind Ivy and Clara what was at stake. Glimmer's safety. Ben's future as an apprentice at Crystal Castle. Bella's debut tomorrow morning.

"Group hug for luck," Ivy said.

The three best friends squeezed each other tight.

"Let's go," Bella said.

Bella led the way to the edge of the Dark Forest. Light peeked through the tall, leafless trees that stretched into the sky. Before she could think about it, Bella veered away from Ivy and Clara. Immediately, the temperature dropped a few degrees. Bella, glad for her cardigan, pulled the gray sleeves down to her knuckles. Ivy's and Clara's footsteps soon disappeared, and the only sounds in the dim forest were Bella's sneakers crunching on twigs and dead leaves.

Mushrooms—red-and-white spotted—bloomed along the base of a massive tree. Roots as big as Bella swirled into the ground. The princess stepped closer to the tree, in awe of the roots, and movement made her jump back.

The tree roots inflated before her eyes, getting thicker and longer. It was as if they were protecting the tree. Bella took a few steps backward and found a semi-path to walk on. Ravens cawed overhead, and their wings fluttered.

Bella swatted at a bug that whined in her ear. Another one of the annoying insects flew in front of her eyes, and she broke into a run. *That was the creepiest bug ever!* she thought. Not only had the insect been the size of her hand, but it had a red body and four hairy, gross legs. Bella had never seen that bug outside of the Dark Forest.

Bella licked her dry lips, wanting to call for Glimmer, but she was too afraid of alerting Queen Fire's spies. The princess wanted to get in and out of the forest as fast as possible. Her parents had forbidden her to enter the dangerous woods ever since she'd been old enough to talk. Now, not only was she in the Dark Forest, but she was without the protection of her unicorn.

Bella's heart thudded so hard in her chest that she was sure the forest creatures could hear her heartbeat. *Please, please don't let me run into one of Queen Fire's unicorns,* she thought. *Let me find Glimmer and take her home.*

Bella stopped, bending down to look at a marking in the dirt. A hoofprint! The sight of it sent the princess's pulse racing. She was on the right track. Or—Bella gulped—she was on the trail of one of Queen Fire's dangerous unicorns. Bella stood, and a rustling noise filtered into her ears. She saw a flash of something—she couldn't even make out the color—and that was all she needed.

Bella broke into a run, ignoring the squawking birds, the ribbiting frogs, and the scary shadows that covered a lot of the trail. Bella reached a line of hedges and halted, peering over the top.

She gasped. "Glimmer!" Bella cried.

The unicorn lifted her purple-tinted head from the ground and pointed her ears in Bella's direction.

Tears started falling from Bella's eyes. "Glimmer, please don't run away. Please let me talk to you."

Bella swiped at the tears on her cheeks as she took slow steps around the hedge. Glimmer stood like a statue—not a flick of her tail or a blink at the princess.

Bella held out her hand and, reaching Glimmer, placed it gently on the unicorn's shoulder.

Glimmer's muscles rippled, and she let out a huge sigh.

"I know you don't want to be my unicorn anymore," Bella said, choking back tears. "Glimmer, I don't want you to be unhappy. I just want you to be safe. Please come home with me. You can stay at the stables and I promise—you'll be released from your duties as my royal unicorn."

Glimmer craned her neck to face Bella. She blinked her giant liquid-brown eyes and stared into Bella's. Bella didn't break eye contact with Glimmer as she moved her hand to the unicorn's muzzle.

Something was happening. Something Bella had never experienced.

"I must be crazy," Bella said to Glimmer. "I must want you to stay my unicorn so bad that I can tell you want that too."

Glimmer nudged Bella's hand with her muzzle.

She let out a quiet, soft snort. Bella's eyes swept over Glimmer's face, and the unicorn's thoughts rushed into her brain. She could read Glimmer's body language. Glimmer was telling Bella exactly what she was thinking.

"Oh, Glimmer," Bella said, shaking her head. "You *want* to be my unicorn? You didn't run away because you didn't like me?"

Again, Glimmer touched Bella. This time she rested her cheek in the princess's palm and looked back into Bella's eyes.

"You were scared of the debut? Oh, Glimmer! You'd never be a disappointment to me or anyone! You're the only unicorn that I want. I've been so worried about you and missing you since you left."

Bella threw her arms around Glimmer. "I understand that you got nervous. Being a royal can be scary. But you'll always have me. We have each other."

Glimmer stretched her neck around so that it rested lightly on Bella's shoulder as she gave her a unicorn hug.

Bella let go and looked into Glimmer's eyes. "Do you really want to come back to the castle and be my unicorn? That really will make you happy?"

Glimmer blinked, and a sweet look flashed in her eyes.

"Hurray!" Bella said. Happy tears pricked her eyes. "Let's get out of this creepy forest and go home."

Glimmer bobbed her head. Bella picked up her crystal from her pocket and squeezed it in her palm. "I need to tell Ivy and Clara to get out of here right away," Bella explained to Glimmer. "We'll meet them outside of the forest."

Bella couldn't resist hugging Glimmer again. She began to speak the words to summon Ivy's and Clara's crystals. "Crystal I hold in my hand," Bella started. As she spoke, Glimmer's head went high into the air. Her nostrils flared, and her tail began to whip back and forth.

Bella lowered the hand that held the crystal. "Glimmer, what's wrong?"

The princess followed Glimmer's gaze into a line of trees just ahead of them. What Bella saw wasn't easy to miss. Out of the trees, a bright-red unicorn with black eyes and a black horn stepped into the clearing. Its head was lowered—and its horn was pointed right at Glimmer.

8

Most Unusual Rescue

"Glimmer," Bella said in a whisper. "Let's just back away. Maybe it won't fight us."

The words had no sooner left Bella's mouth than the red unicorn swept its ears back and let out a thundering neigh. It had to have been heard throughout the entire forest.

Glimmer nudged Bella beside her, and the princess shrank into her unicorn's coat.

They had no way out.

The red unicorn's black eyes narrowed on Glimmer, and Bella's unicorn bared her teeth. Bella knew Glimmer would fight as hard as necessary to protect her. But she didn't want Glimmer getting hurt. Queen Fire's unicorns were unusually strong and filled with rage. The enemy unicorn struck the earth with a front hoof and lowered its head to charge.

"Enough!"

A familiar voice echoed through the forest.

The red unicorn lifted its head, relaxing its ears, and began backing out of the clearing.

Bella almost fell as she witnessed the unicorn disappearing back into the Dark Forest. Glimmer maintained alert mode, and both she and Bella watched as their unexpected rescuer strode into the clearing.

"Queen Fire," Bella said, trying to keep her voice from shaking.

"You and your precious unicorn are in *my* woods, darling niece," the evil queen said.

Queen Fire looked exactly as she had when

she'd made an unwelcome appearance at Bella's eighth birthday. Red lipstick stained her lips. Long, wavy black hair flowed past her shoulders, and the ends were dyed bright red. She looked nothing like her sister, Bella's mother. Queen Fire's eyes were an endless pit of black.

Her long black dress dragged along the ground, and a red cape was tied across the queen's shoulders. She stopped where her unicorn had pawed the ground and smiled at Bella.

The smile held no warmth. It didn't reach her eyes.

"Why did you save us?" Bella asked. "You stopped your unicorn from attacking."

The queen laughed. "It was not out of sheer devotion and love for you, Princess." The queen tapped a long red fingernail against her cheek. "You haven't spent enough time around your aunt to know how my world—the real world—works.

I saved you and your precious unicorn not just because you are my family, but because it will benefit *me*."

Queen Fire's words made Bella's stomach drop. Being around this woman was almost scarier than facing one of her unicorns. Glimmer shared Bella's thinking, and Bella felt Glimmer's muscles tighten under her hand.

"What do you want?" Bella asked. She summoned every ounce of courage left in her body. "I owe you for your protection. *I* want to repay the debt. If you even think Glimmer is part of any deal, you're wrong."

The queen stared. The forest was silent. Bella felt as though she'd stopped breathing. Then Queen Fire burst into laughter.

"Oh, my Bella!" Queen Fire said, grinning. "You may have a purple aura, dear, but you have the courage of your black-auraed aunt."

"I told you the first time we met," Bella said. "I'm nothing like you!"

Queen Fire's smile left her face. "Time will tell, Princess. You can't control what's inside of you. There may be untapped evil you've yet to even imagine."

Bella gritted her teeth. She had to get Glimmer out of here. It wasn't going to do any good to keep arguing with Queen Fire.

"Please just tell me what you want," Bella said.

The queen folded her arms. "I don't know when I'll want something from you or what that may be. But I agree that you, Princess Bella, are in my debt. When I am ready for you to fulfill my favor, you will know."

The queen smiled again, making Bella's knees shake even harder.

"I—," Bella started.

A loud *crack!* cut her off, and black smoke rose

from the spot where Queen Fire had just stood.

"Let's go! Right now!" Bella said to Glimmer. Glimmer turned in the direction Bella had entered the clearing, clearly beckoning Bella to follow.

Without a look back, the two raced out of the Dark Forest and into the waiting open arms of Ivy and Clara.

9

Not-So-Secret Plan Anymore

"I can't believe Queen Fire saved you!" Ivy said.

"I'm just glad we found you, Glimmer," Clara said, patting the unicorn's neck. The three friends and Glimmer walked over the castle's drawbridge. On the walk back to the castle, Bella had told them about her run-in with Queen Fire in the woods. Both girls had been scared and worried about what happened—and Bella's debt to the queen—but at the end of the talk, they had been grateful Bella's aunt had chosen to stop the unicorn fight.

"Uh-oh," Bella said.

Her parents, Frederick, and Ben stood in front

of the stables. Ben's head was down, and Queen Katherine's arms were crossed.

"Bella, how long were you planning to keep it a secret that your unicorn had gone missing?" King Phillip asked. His voice was low and very serious.

"I'm sorry," Bella said. "But please don't send Ben away! This wasn't his fault. I made him promise not to tell anyone."

"Ben should have come to me," Frederick said. "However, I am the stable manager. It is my responsibility to make sure that all the royal unicorns are safe. I should have asked Ben about Glimmer the moment I began to feel it was odd that I hadn't seen her in a while."

Bella's stomach twisted and turned. Ben couldn't leave because of her!

"How did you find out?" Bella asked, her voice quiet.

"Frederick came to your father and me," Queen Katherine said. "He hadn't seen Glimmer, and with Ben at the stables and both you and Glimmer gone, Frederick was worried that you were out riding alone."

"We came down to the stables immediately," King Phillip continued. "Ben was so worried about you and your friends being in the Dark Forest that he told us the truth. We were moments away from sending out every guard at the castle."

Bella glanced at Ben. He mouthed, "I'm sorry." She shook her head at him.

"Mom, Dad," Bella said. "I'm sorry that I've been lying to you. I should have told you the second that I realized Glimmer had escaped. I know you must have been really worried about me, Ivy, and Clara in the Dark Forest."

"Yes, we were," Queen Katherine said. "Bella, your father and I will discuss this with you tonight.

It's quite serious that you lied and went to a place we forbade you from going."

Bella nodded. "Okay," she said in a whisper.

"Ivy and Clara," King Phillip said, "please go with Ben. He'll ready a carriage to take you both home."

The girls quietly thanked the king and queen and disappeared into the stables with Ben.

"I know you're mad," Bella said. "But please don't make Ben leave Crystal Castle."

The grown-ups exchanged looks. Bella's hand that was tangled in Glimmer's mane was sweaty.

"We are grateful to Ben for telling the truth," King Phillip said. "He also helped keep you safe." The king looked at Frederick. "Ben is welcome to stay as your apprentice if that's what you wish."

Bella held her breath as she watched Frederick.

"He may stay," Frederick finally answered.

"Thank you, Frederick!" Bella cheered.

"Go get Glimmer settled in," Queen Katherine said. "Then come straight inside."

"I will, Mom," Bella said. "Thank you."

A few minutes later she hugged Glimmer again, never wanting to let go. The royal unicorn was safe and secure in her stall. It was just Bella, Glimmer, and Ben.

"Are you ever going to let go of Glimmer?" Ben asked. He smiled and leaned against the stall door jamb. Bella had told Ben about running into Queen Fire. Like Ivy and Clara, he had been upset. But he was beyond relieved that Bella and Glimmer were home safe.

"Nah, I think I'll hold on to Glimmer until I'm fifteen," Bella said, only half-teasing.

"Only until you're *fifteen*?" Ben asked. "Jeez, Bella. That's giving up pretty early. I thought you'd at least hang on until forty."

They both laughed. Glimmer seemed to sense

the lift in mood. She threw up her head and shook her mane. The purple-tinted strands swished against the top of Bella's shoulder and tickled her cheek.

"Fine, fine," Bella said, pretend-sighing. "I guess I can do forty."

Ben grinned and looked down, swirling his boot on the concrete aisle. "Seriously," he started. "I have to thank you again for everything you did for me."

"You don't have to keep thanking me," Bella said. "Really. You've been so great to Glimmer and me since you got here. It wouldn't have been fair for you to get in trouble."

Ben slowly shook his head and let out a breath. "I almost can't believe Glimmer is back and that we pulled it off." He turned his gaze to the unicorn. "I'm going to set up twenty more cameras and cast a dozen spells to make sure you sleep tight, Glimmer."

Glimmer nudged Bella's shoulder. Bella looked into Glimmer's eyes, and what she saw made her feel warm from head to toe.

"I don't think Glimmer's going anywhere," Bella said. She lightly kissed Glimmer's cheek, and the unicorn let out a soft *whoosh* of breath.

"I think it's time we both got some rest," Bella said to Glimmer. "We've got a big day tomorrow."

Glimmer rested her soft muzzle in Bella's hands. She looked into the princess's eyes, and Bella knew that she would be able to sleep well tonight—Glimmer was happy to be home.

10

Glimmer's Big Debut

"Glimmer!" Bella cried, waking and sitting up in bed. Her heart thudded against her chest, as if she had just run laps around the castle's moat.

Glimmer's home, Bella reminded herself. She let out a breath as if trying to exhale the nightmare. She'd been dreaming that Glimmer had been captured by Queen Fire. Goose bumps ran up and down her arms as she remembered the queen's promise to collect on Bella's debt. *But Glimmer's safe from my deal,* the princess reminded herself. *It could be six days or six years before Queen Fire wants something from me.* She took a long, deep breath through her nose. When she exhaled, she pushed all of the thoughts of Queen Fire from her mind. Bella was going to try her hardest not to think about her aunt. At least not today.

Bella yanked back the purple-and-white-striped sheets and comforter and ran to her window. She undid the latch and pushed it open. Her view from the tower was perfect. She could see the stables, pastures, and barnyard. Ben and Frederick emerged from the stables with a gorgeous purple-splashed unicorn in tow. The view instantly made her happy.

Glimmer! Bella thought. *You really are home and safe.*

Through her window, Bella watched as Ben turned Glimmer in a circle and tied her to one of the white fence rails. Frederick carried over a bucket filled with brushes, and Ben began to ready Glimmer for her debut. Bella closed her eyes, trying to clear her mind of anything but her connection to Glimmer. The princess felt happiness, excitement, and a touch of nerves. Bella opened her eyes, grinning. Glimmer's feelings matched her own!

"Good morning, Bella!" Lyssa entered Bella's room. She had a garment bag in one hand.

Bella eyed the bag. "Jeez, Lyss. I thought you were never going to get here."

"Ha, ha," Lyssa said, winking. "That's talk, coming from someone still in her pj's."

"Didn't you hear?" Bella asked, putting a hand on her hip. "Pajamas are *so* in this season. Everyone is wearing them all the time."

Lyssa grinned. "Oh, well then, you won't want the clothes your mom gave me for your debut." She took the black garment bag and started to put it in Bella's closet.

"Um, wait!" Bella said, hurrying over to Lyssa. "The pj's all day is totally a fad. I'm going to stay fashion forward and wear real clothes during the day."

Lyssa laughed. "Wow! What perfect timing, since I brought this!"

Bella watched as Lyssa unzipped the clothing bag. Carefully Lyssa took out a pair of shimmery gold leggings, a plum-purple tee with lace-edged sleeves and hem, and black riding boots. A gold chain with a prancing unicorn pendant hung from the hanger.

"You like?" Lyssa asked.

"I love!" Bella said. "These clothes are perfect for today."

Lyssa helped her change. The castle was quiet when Bella left and headed for the stables to meet her parents.

The king and queen had spoken to Bella for a *long* time last night about the Glimmer situation. Bella had realized that if she had told her parents from the start, she would have probably found Glimmer faster. King Phillip had reminded Bella that what happened wasn't Ben's fault, and if he and Bella had told the truth earlier, then they wouldn't have had to worry about Ben's future at the castle. Most of all, though, the king and queen were relieved that their daughter and Glimmer were home safe.

"Ben!" Bella called, spotting him in the stable yard.

"Hi, Bella," he said, smiling. "My uncle's holding Glimmer. He asked me to keep an eye out for you."

"There's one *huge* problem!" Bella said. She looked over her shoulder to make sure no one else was around. "I haven't actually ridden Glimmer before. Now I have to ride her to the town square and be in front of the entire kingdom!"

Ben tapped his index finger against one of his temples. "One step ahead of you, Princess."

Bella clutched her hands together. "Really?"

"Really. Frederick knows that you haven't had riding lessons, so I asked him if I could lead Glimmer for the debut."

"Ben!" Bella hugged him quickly. "That's only the best plan *ever*! You're a genius!"

Ben shook his head. "Just a *very* smart apprentice." He grinned. "So, Princess Bella, may I assist you during your debut?"

"Hmmm." Bella rolled her eyes to the sky, pretending to think. "*Yes!* Thank you, Ben!"

Ben bowed his head. He waved a hand in the direction of the stable yard. "This way, Princess Bella. It's time for your first ride." He whispered the last sentence, and he and Bella exchanged secret smiles.

Bella half skipped after Ben. She wanted the kingdom to love Glimmer as much as she did. But right now, what she wanted more than anything was to *finally* ride her unicorn. Bella's boots crunched on gravel, and Glimmer turned her head in Bella's direction. Two pricked ears pointed toward Bella, and Glimmer let out a soft whinny.

Bella hurried over, and Frederick laughed and he moved out of the way as the princess threw her arms around Glimmer's neck. The unicorn smelled like sweet hay and daisies. Superfine strands of clear wire had been twisted throughout Glimmer's mane and tail. The wires shimmered and slowly changed from pink to green to purple—they ran through *every* color that Bella had ever seen in Crystal Kingdom! Glimmer's white coat glittered in the sun, and it reminded Bella of pixie dust.

"You look *so* pretty!" Bella told Glimmer. The princess looked into Glimmer's eyes and saw love and happiness. The princess knew *she* would do anything to protect her unicorn in return.

Bella perched on her tiptoes and leaned close

to Glimmer's right ear. "Nothing's ever made me feel more like a princess."

"May I help you up?" Frederick asked.

"Please!" Bella said. *I get to finally ride!* she thought.

Frederick motioned for Bella to follow him as he led Glimmer over to a set of three wooden stairs.

"Climb on up and put your left foot here," Frederick said. He held a triangle-shaped iron with a rubber grip at the bottom. The triangle's bottom supported Bella's weight. Bella followed the stable manager's instructions and lowered herself onto the leather saddle.

Frederick quickly explained how Bella would use her hands and feet to guide Glimmer.

"That's a lot to remember," Bella said. Her heart beat a little faster.

"Ben will be right there, so don't worry,"

Frederick said. He patted her knee, smiling as he waved to Ben.

Ben hurried over and took the rainbow-striped rope from Frederick.

"Oh, Bella!" Queen Katherine, arm in arm with King Phillip, beamed at her daughter. "You look perfect with Glimmer. Phillip, take a photo!"

Bella's dad already had the camera lens pointed at the princess and Glimmer. Bella grinned into the camera. "Unicorn!" she said, giggling.

After a few more photos, the king and queen climbed into the Royal Carriage. The beautiful carriage, powered by the sun, glowed bright despite the sun being out in full force.

With a smile at Bella, Ben led Glimmer forward through the stable yard, across the drawbridge, and out onto the private winding Royal Road to town.

The shimmering purple strands in Glimmer's

mane and tail complemented the crystal-flecked path under her hooves. Glimmer pranced toward town, and Bella couldn't stop grinning.

"Ben?" Bella asked. "What if the crowds scare Glimmer? She's never been around so many people before."

"Again," Ben said, smiling, "got you covered."

Soon they were in town. Ben led Glimmer down a path secured by a few Royal Guards and into the town square. High in the air, a giant red sign flashed QUIET, PLEASE! and NEW ROYAL UNICORN! CAUTION!

"My uncle came here before we got here," Ben explained, looking up at the signs. "He asked the crowd not to wave any signs or make any noise that might scare Glimmer. She's new to everything. But soon the people won't even faze her."

Dozens of people, held back by a shield spell, smiled, held up cameras, or whispered to each other as Ben halted Glimmer. Bella looked over her shoulder for her parents. The king and queen emerged from the Royal Carriage and greeted the people of Crystal Kingdom with waves and smiles.

Bella recognized a few reporters from the local newspaper as they scribbled in notepads and had cameras on tripods that recorded the event. She looked over the crowd, and two hands shot into the air. Clara and Ivy! Bella waved at her besties.

The king and queen stood on the podium that towered above the crowd. Bella couldn't help but flash back to her dad standing there, sword at his side, when Queen Fire had scared the crowd on her birthday. The evil queen's words from yesterday made Bella shiver.

Immediately, Glimmer's ears swept back toward Bella, and she struck the ground with a front hoof.

"Easy, girl," Ben said, petting Glimmer. "You okay?" he asked Bella.

"Totally fine. Just thought about yesterday for a second," Bella said.

Ben half smiled. "Look around. Maybe the fact that, oh, a *few* people showed up will distract you."

Bella laughed. "That helps! Plus, we're here on a school day."

"I'm not exactly sad about school being canceled," Ben said. He led Glimmer toward the crowd and turned her in a big circle so everyone could see.

"People of Crystal Kingdom," King Phillip's voice came through a microphone.

Everyone's heads swiveled in his direction. Even Glimmer's!

"Thank you all for joining my family on this beautiful day," the king said. "Queen Katherine

115

and I are thrilled to introduce you to our daughter's unicorn. Princess Bella is now paired with Glimmer."

Chills ran up and down Bella's arms. She leaned forward and patted Glimmer's shoulder. The unicorn bowed her neck in appreciation, letting out a soft whicker.

"Together, let us all welcome Glimmer as a member of the royal family and of Crystal Kingdom," King Phillip said.

The crowd raised their hands in the air as Bella's smile grew. The overhead red sign flashed green to GENTLE APPLAUSE, and cheers broke out across the square.

"See what you would have missed?" Bella asked Glimmer.

The princess leaned forward, hugging Glimmer. Cameras clicked, and the crowd clapped harder.

"Welcome home," Bella said.

Glimmer craned her neck around, a twinkle in her eyes, and bumped Bella's boot with her nose. Bella's heart soared higher than the podium. Glimmer was definitely here to stay!

Green with Envy

"Next Friday is going to be the best day *ever*!" Princess Bella said to her two best friends. Ivy and Clara walked beside Bella as the three girls left their classroom on Friday afternoon. The girls had school every day at Crystal Castle—Bella's home—and shared the classroom with six other third-grade students. Most of them, like Ivy, had parents who worked at Crystal Castle. Another student, older by a year, was Ben. His uncle ran the royal stables. Bella's closest friends weren't official "royals," but they were princesses to her!

"I know! I love spring break!" Ivy said. "No

school for an entire week!" She slung her pink shimmery backpack over one shoulder. Pieces of her white-blond hair were twisted and held off her face by several rhinestone butterfly hair clips. The enchanted butterfly wings fluttered open and shut, making the gemstones sparkle.

"That's *so* exciting, but I'm with Bella," Clara said. "Friday is huge!" Clara, the most outgoing of the three friends, skipped ahead a couple of steps, then turned around and walked backward so she faced her friends. Clara's backpack, covered in teensy blue lights that flashed on when the bag moved, rolled beside her on wheels over the castle's marble floor.

Bella and Ivy giggled at Clara as she almost tripped over her own feet.

"My parents didn't even tell me that they were going to throw a party for our class," Bella said. "We get the whole week off, and on Friday is the party, with a movie in the garden, desserts, and music. And we all get to hang out."

Bella smiled at the thought of spending more time with her classmates. Lately, the princess had barely enough time to see her besties and her new friend, Ben. Ben had just joined Bella's class when he had come to Crystal Castle to be an apprentice for his uncle Frederick. Frederick was the royal stable manager, and he had put Ben to work helping care for the castle's prized unicorns, including Bella's own unicorn, Glimmer.

"Plus, there's an *extra* surprise that I didn't tell you about yet," Bella said mysteriously.

Clara stopped so suddenly that Bella and Ivy almost plowed into her.

"Spill!" Clara said, her long honey-blond waves swishing around her shoulders.

"Tell us!" Ivy added, making wide eyes and pouting.

Bella laughed. "Okay. Want to go to the stables? We could sit with Glimmer and talk. We already got the okay from your parents for you to stay after school for a while."

"Stables. Yes! Let's go! I want to know the extra surprise!" Clara said, grabbing the hands of Ivy and Bella and pulling them forward.

They ran, laughing, down a long hallway in the castle. The girls stopped in front of the giant wooden front door, and Clara told her backpack to "stay." Ivy put hers beside Clara's, and Bella dropped her own purple one on the pile.

A castle security guard, gleaming sword at his side, opened the door for them. Bright sunlight almost blinded Bella for a moment as she skipped with her friends across the Crystal Castle lawn toward the stables.

Bella carefully looked over the grounds. She wanted everything to be perfect for her surprise.

But there wasn't a thing she would change. Royal unicorns, white as fresh snow, munched on emerald-colored grass in pastures on both sides of the castle's driveway. A few unicorns were napping—flat out on their sides—and soaking up the sun. The weather was perfect—warm but not too hot. It was Bella's favorite time of year.

The girls reached the stables and slowed to a walk so they didn't scare any of the unicorns. The royal stables had a mint-green exterior and a black roof.

Inside, a large main aisle had a row of stalls on either side. Since it was so nice out, most of the stalls were empty, as the unicorns were outside. But at the end of the left aisle, a closed stall door held one *very* special unicorn. Bella craned her neck, looking for Ben,

"Glimmer!" Bella called. "We're here!"

She couldn't help but smile when her beautiful

unicorn stuck her head over the stall door. The purple tinted unicorn neighed excitedly when she saw Bella.

Bella slid the giant bolt on the stall door and opened it. Ivy and Clara followed her inside, shutting the door behind them.

"Hi, Glimmer," Bella said softly. "Pretty girl." The princess hugged Glimmer's neck while Ivy and Clara petted her.

Glimmer bumped her velvet-soft nose against Bella's hands, making the princess laugh.

Bella and Glimmer shared a very special bond. Just under a week ago, Glimmer had disappeared from the royal stables. At first Bella had been certain her unicorn had been uni-napped, until she got help from Ben, Ivy, and Clara. They learned that Glimmer had run away, and after days of searching, Bella had found Glimmer deep in the scary Dark Forest. The princess had pleaded with Glimmer to follow her out the dangerous woods. She wanted Glimmer to be safe, even if Glimmer didn't want to be her unicorn.

As Glimmer had nudged Bella's hands just now, it was something the unicorn had done in the woods. When Glimmer touched Bella, something magical happened between them. Bella was able to read Glimmer's body language and, almost like mind reading, be able to tell what Glimmer was thinking or how she was feeling.

That day, surrounded by the Dark Forest, Glimmer had told Bella that she was scared to be the princess's unicorn. Glimmer loved Bella more than anything, but worried she wouldn't be good enough.

Bella assured Glimmer that the unicorn was perfect and everything she wanted.

Princess Bella jumped, startled, as Glimmer bumped her hands a little harder.

"It's like Glimmer's saying, 'Earth to Bella,'" Ivy said with a smile.

"True. She's also saying, 'Get me a treat, please,'" Bella said.

She ran a hand down Glimmer's white neck with her light-purple-tinged mane. "I'll get you one before we leave, okay?"

Glimmer bobbed her head.

The girls settled onto the clean straw and Glimmer, not wanting to be left out, folded her legs under her and delicately lowered herself to the stall floor.

"Aw! I *have* to take a picture of this even though I don't have my camera," Clara said. She made a rectangle shape with her fingers, touching her pointer fingers to her thumbs. Photos were always better with a camera, but magic worked in a pinch. "Photograph," she commanded. She closed one eye and moved her hands closer to Glimmer. "Take picture now."

Click!

A small burst of sparkles shimmered into the air. The photo appeared in the air and Ivy and Clara tilted their heads to see it.

"Aw!" Bella said. "Send me that picture."

Clara nodded. "I will. Camera, I'm finished." The image of Glimmer vanished.

"So do you guys remember my cousin Violet?" Bella asked.

"She's a princess in Foris Kingdom, right?" Ivy asked. "A few months younger than us?"

Foris Kingdom was on one of four sky islands—pieces of land that floated way above the clouds. A person could only reach another island if a rainbow or moonbow was cast. Then, the sky island was in walking distance.

"Right," Bella said. "Violet's dad is my uncle, King Alexander—my dad's brother. You guys know how close Violet and I are. Even though she lives in

Foris, we've been like best friends since we could walk."

"You've talked a lot about her," Clara said. "She sounds so nice."

Bella smiled. "She is. We have bonded even more since my pair to Glimmer."

"That makes sense," Ivy said. "Did Violet want to know all about your pairing? I know I would."

Bella nodded. "I told her most of it over the phone." Bella sighed. "I really wish you could meet her."

Ivy and Clara both frowned, sticking out their bottom lips.

"We would have so much fun together," Bella said. "And we will, because . . . Violet's coming to visit! Surprise!"

Mermaid Tales

*Exciting under-the-sea adventures
with Shelly and her mermaid friends!*

Candy Fairies

Chocolate Dreams

Rainbow Swirl

Caramel Moon

Cool Mint

Magic Hearts

Gooey Goblins

The Sugar Ball

A Valentine's Surprise

Bubble Gum Rescue

Double Dip

Jelly Bean Jumble

The Chocolate Rose

A Royal Wedding

Marshmallow Mystery

Visit candyfairies.com for more delicious fun with your favorite fairies.

Play games, download activities, and so much more!